The Bug Club!

Fanciful Fantasies for
Bright Children

by
Mary Dawn

First Printing

ISBN (13): 978-0692307779

ISBN (10): 069230777X

Printed in the United States of America
    JustUs Press
    P O Box 97124
    Lakewood WA 98497

CONTENTS

iv | Mary Dawn

DEDICATION

Dedicated to my own children

David

Rick

Joy

Emma

Paul

And the memory of Tom

All of my children, grandchildren and
great-grandchildren are very bright children
— which is why they love my stories.
I invite you to enjoy them too!

The Adventures of
Bristol Beasterly

Bristol Beasterly is a spider —
not your ordinary everyday,
plain house spider. Oh no. Bristol is
a descendant of the Royal Family Beasterly. In
particular, Bristol is the direct offspring of the
famous Gaylord Farquar Beasterly, who was
well known for his European adventures and
daring escapades... but that is another story.

Therefore, don't be surprised to find anything
unusual about Bristol's daring, dangerous, and no
doubt exaggerated adventures.

To begin at the beginning, Bristol Beasterly's
mother was none other than the world-famous

Maude Rose Beasterly, noted for her beautiful webs. At the fair, she won many prizes for her webs, in both design and speed of production. Also, it is said (not too loudly) that her webs far surpassed Grandmother Neusbaum's webs. And we all thought that Grandmother Neusbaum was The Best!

Maude Rose outdid herself constructing the web that would be the home for her children. She wove into it many new designs never before seen (nor has anyone seen them since). In one corner she carefully laid her eggs, wrapped snugly in her very best material and fastened securely to the south wall of the Vanderfellers' garage. Throughout the web she gently placed flies and larvae, working them into beautiful designs of flowers, ferns, and funny, fascinating frameworks.

Bristol spent the first weeks of life working free of the birthing shell. Once free, Bristol announced to no one in particular, "There now, I'm off for an adventure."

Bristol crept forth carefully and slowly, inching along all sides of the web, always heeding Mother's warning not to go beyond the edge. Bristol examined every inch of the well-designed web, tasting a bit of every delicacy that Maude Rose, Bristol's mother, had placed there.

Now, while this may have been enough for Bristol's brothers and sisters, we must not forget that Bristol had inherited the ancestors' adventuresome spirit. It was not long before the confines of the web were not enough of the world for the descendant of Gaylord Farquar Beasterly.

Bristol's determination — and many days of practice — resulted in the ability to wear a facial expression of resolution by forming a just-so mouth shape and form a spinneret into a very small "o". By straining a tiny wee bit, he began to spin small webs. Oh, nothing as elaborate and elegant as Maude Rose's webs, but they were sturdy and serviceable.

Making the spinneret much, much smaller, Bristol learned to carefully spin one veerryy long thread. By putting the thread over the side of the web, Bristol could swing by the hour, back and forth, forth and back, higher and higher. Even though Mother called warning after warning, young Bristol was enjoying the adventure too much to pay attention.

After three days of such swinging, Bristol became bored with the game and experimented by making a strand of thread long enough to reach the window. Then another, just a l-i-t-t-l-e bit longer, long enough to reach Mr. Vanderfeller's workbench. "What great fun," squealed Bristol.

Great fun, that is, until Mrs. Vanderfeller came out of the house holding a broom. As she swept by, the broom handle caught Bristol's thread and broke it, leaving the bewildered spider stranded on a corner of the workbench. Luckily for Bristol, Mrs. Vanderfeller didn't see what happened, or the "Adventures of Bristol

Beasterly" would have ended right then and there. As it happened, Bristol crept carefully around the hammer, across the saw (almost losing a leg), and hid behind a jar of nails until Mrs. Vanderfeller left.

Bristol's brothers and sisters made a terrible spider racket, shouting warnings and calling for Bristol to come back. But no, Bristol was not interested in going back. This was an adventure!

All the Beasterly children had heard tragic stories of their cousin Happy Hopperfield, and they knew the dangers of the big world. Why, when Happy was very young, they found... but, that's another story.

After many hours, Maude Rose gave up peering over the side of the web to see what her adventuresome offspring was doing. Bristol noticed and crawled out of the hiding place. "Hey, look at me, all on my own."

Crawling carefully across the workbench, Bristol's feet experienced first the roughness of the file, then the scratchy sandpaper. Proceeding through a paint brush, Bristol felt the tickling sensation. Then came a pane of glass. "This is more like it; this feels so smooth it makes my feet feel better," Bristol exclaimed.

Just as the little spider began to enjoy skating on the glass, out of the house came Mr. Vanderfeller. When he spied Bristol, he immediately picked up a fly swatter and brought it above his head, preparing to bring it down on... oh no! He was aiming right at Bristol's beautiful young head!

Moving faster than Bristol had ever moved before, in a flurry and a scurry, the little spider arrived at the edge of the glass, spun a short thread, and pitched recklessly over the side — landing right in the middle of the toolbox.

Since Mr. Vanderfeller couldn't see very well, he didn't see where Bristol had gone. He put down the fly swatter, picked up his toolbox, and went into the house to fix a chair leg.

Bristol had never been inside a house
before. There had been stories, however, about
Great Aunt Alice who, while spinning her web
in a living room corner, had been swept... but
we'll have to wait for that story.

Bristol crawled slowly out of the toolbox and
onto the kitchen table. In the center sat a large,
potted plant, the likes of which Bristol had
never seen. What a place for an adventure!
Scurrying to the pot, Bristol crept very carefully
up the side. It was slow going, but Bristol kept
at it, finally reaching the top and dropping over
the edge into... "Why, this must be dirt," said
Bristol. There were stories about Wiggly
Wormly who was born in dirt under a lilac bush.
Ah, ah, ah... later.

Bristol spent many enjoyable hours playing
in the dirt, making small webs and just feeling
the softness of the soil. What a wonderful place
to...

"What's this?" asked Bristol. Suddenly,
water had come pouring over the little spider,

making it so... gasp... difficult to... breathe. Of course Bristol couldn't swim. It was a desperate spider who felt the water deepen and who grabbed wildly at a passing leaf. Catching the edge, Bristol pulled himself up and stayed very, very still for a very, very long time, trying to breathe properly again. As the water settled, Bristol shook all eight legs and dried off, using the leaf as a towel. My, what a lovely adventure. Now I need a place to spend the night.

Gathering courage, Bristol spun a very fine thread and swung down from the table onto a curtain (barely catching the end of it) and scurried across the window sill. Bristol turned slowly and surveyed the room, spotting an organ. Now Bristol didn't know what the organ was, or what it was used for, but tired and seeking a comfortable, dark, dry place to spend the night seemed enough. Thus, a short trip by thread took the weary spider to this temporary "bedroom". Immediately, sleep took over.

A few moments later, a soft, low, and rather lovely sound gently woke Bristol from sleep. Someone was making music on the organ. Rising to a great crescendo, the sound turned deafening. Oh my, thought Bristol as the throbbing reached the frail spider body. What is that ringing in my head? No longer pleasant, the "bedroom" was abandoned. Too tired to go far, Bristol lay shaking on the carpet for a moment, then curled up all eight legs and went back to sleep.

The next morning Bristol awoke to find Jack, the family dog, lying with its paw oh-so-close to Bristol's head. You remember how daring and brave Bristol could be? Well, Bristol carefully crept onto the soft fur of Jack's paw and proceeded up the front leg. How lovely the fur felt to the spider's feet; and how it did tickle his nose! If Bristol could make it up... to... the... collar... just a bit more... and... no! No! Don't scratch! Hold on, Bristol!

When the dog became quiet again, Bristol slipped under its collar and proceeded to make himself secure with a strong thread. Bristol waited for the ride that was to come. He didn't have to wait long. For the rest of that day he rode back and forth, forth and back, through the house. Once they even went outside where Bristol enjoyed a very fast ride while Jack chased the family cat.

Whew! By nightfall, both Jack and Bristol were tired. When Jack returned to the garage to sleep, Bristol took a long leap and landed... right in the front seat of the family car. Checking every available spot to rest, he chose a place behind the sun visor. Encircled by a finely spun web, Bristol Beasterly fell asleep.

In the morning, Bristol awoke to all kinds of hustle and bustle. Mr. and Mrs. Vanderfeller were preparing for a trip. This seemed a very good idea to Bristol. Another adventure! He had no suitcase to pack, but he did need to finish a very fine, strong web and catch a big, juicy fly (to weave into an intricate pattern just like Mother had taught).

Bristol had a glorious time for the next few days, catching all kinds of different and exotic bugs in the fine web. Never had Bristol tasted such flavors before.

One day in mid-afternoon as Mrs. Vanderfeller was driving, Bristol heard Mr. Vanderfeller remark, "This is Death Valley, one of the hottest parts of the desert." Bristol wondered what a desert was. Curious, the spider went to the edge of the visor and leaned over as far as possible to see. But it wasn't far enough. Spinning a tiny thread, Bristol jumped. For the first time, the spider had been too excited to make sure the thread was secure and, sure enough, down went Bristol, losing all control and landing in Mrs. Vanderfeller's lap.

Who was more surprised?

Mrs. Vanderfeller, acting out of fear, smacked Bristol right on top of the spider's head and picked up the stunned creature and sent him flying out the open window. Luckily, Bristol landed on the side of the road, just off the pavement, rolled over twice, and came to rest at the base of a large cactus.

Shaken, but unhurt, Bristol got up, brushed off some sand, and looked around. What a wonderful place for an adventure! Ah, but that's another story.

NOTE TO PARENTS:

Next time you read this story to your child, stop at one of those "this is another story" places and ask your offspring to imagine a story. For instance, "Can you imagine what happened to Bristol's cousin, Happy Hopperfield who wanted to see the world?"

Frieda Firefly

Young Jasper was lost. He sat down on a log in the forest and put his head in his hands. What was he to do? It was getting dark and the other Boy Scouts would soon miss him. Jasper thought about last year and his first camping trip with the Scouts. He was ten years old then, and already loved camping and hiking. The Scoutmaster had taught them all about nature and camping.

They had been sitting around the campfire that night when Jasper noticed tiny flashing lights at the edge of the woods. The Scoutmaster explained that the lights were tiny little fireflies, sometimes called lightning bugs.

The boys quickly ran to their tents to get their bug-catching cans and jars. They caught enough bugs in each jar to light their way back to their tents. Jasper, along with most of the boys, freed his fireflies when he reached the tent.

As he turned to enter the tent, Jasper tripped over another bug jar. One of the boys had dropped the jar with the lightning bugs trapped inside. Jasper knelt and released the lid. Out flew all of the bugs except one.

"Oh, you're hurt," said Jasper, gently reaching into the jar to pick up the injured firefly. He laid the firefly in the palm of his hand and looked at it closely. He couldn't see much by the moonlight, and commented, "We'll just have to wait until morning."

Inside the tent, Jasper made a little bed for the firefly out of his neckerchief, placed his firefly friend on it, and slipped it under the cot.

Who was this little firefly friend? you may ask. And what was it doing in that jar?

The firefly was named Frieda. She was born in those very woods and began to glow while still in her egg stage. She practiced very hard to control her chemicals (which cause her to glow). When Frieda came out of her egg stage, she was very beautiful — black with tiny red and yellow spots. Her body measured about a half-inch long, and she was eager to play with the other fireflies. She loved flying up and down and all around the big oak tree at the edge of the woods.

Frieda had many firefly friends. They spent each night flying up and down, blinking their lights at one another. (Once Frieda heard about a relative in South America who was rumored to have glowed such a beautiful green color that a human lady made a tiny harness for her and pinned Frieda's relative to her dress for decoration!)

One night when Frieda was happily flying around the oak tree as usual, she forgot to watch where she was going. Frieda flew right into a raspberry bush and became so tangled she couldn't free herself, try as she might. She blinked and blinked her light, but no one seemed to notice.

Frieda started to cry, but soon realized that crying wouldn't help, and might even short-circuit her light. She stopped. Calmly, she mixed her chemicals and, patiently, she blinked harder and brighter, over and over again.

Sure enough, one of Frieda's friends, Lisa Lightning Bug, flew by, saw the trouble her friend was in, and quickly flew off for help. She brought back many fireflies, who pushed and pulled the raspberry bush until Frieda was free. She thanked them all with a blink of her body and flew home to rest.

The very next night, the adventuresome Frieda was caught — again. This time it was in a Boy Scout's bug-catching jar. As the Scout put the lid back on the jar, it struck one of Frieda's legs and bent her wing. "Oh dear, oh dear," thought Frieda. "What am I to do now?" When the other fireflies were released, Frieda lay helpless in the jar. Exhausted, she fell asleep.

When Frieda awoke, she found herself lying on a tiny blue bed — Jasper's neckerchief. The Boy Scout, waking about the same time, remembered the little firefly and reached under his cot. He picked up Frieda, bed and all, and held her in his hand. "I see now what is the matter," Jasper whispered. "Your left wing is bent and your leg must hurt."

Jasper smoothed the wing flat again as best he could. Frieda felt a slight pain, but didn't cry. "There now," said Jasper. "I think rest is what you need." He placed Frieda gently onto his pillow where Frieda stayed all day, glad for the chance to heal.

Jasper dressed, went to eat breakfast, and began another exciting day at camp. That evening when Jasper returned to his tent, he went right to the bed. He didn't expect to find the little firefly, but there she was, right on the pillow where he had left her. She lay fast asleep.

After dark, Frieda tested her blinking apparatus. She glowed two weak flickers of light. Still sore from last night's experience, she tried one more time to blink, turned over, and went back to sleep.

The second morning when Frieda awoke, she felt much better. Carefully, she tried her wings. "They work," she exclaimed. "Thank goodness, they work!" She flew around Jasper's head and settled on his shoulder. After all, Jasper was her friend; he had saved her life. Frieda rode around on Jasper's shoulder all morning.

The Scouts were free after lunch to do what they wanted. This was just the chance Jasper was waiting for. With Frieda hanging onto his collar, he returned to the half-light of the tent. He had an idea. Now maybe, just maybe, he could teach his firefly friend to count, using her light. "One," Jasper said as he turned his flashlight on and off one time. "Two," he continued as the flashlight blinked twice.

"Three," Jasper said, this time blinking the flashlight three times. Frieda tried, but she wasn't used to controlling both timing and chemicals at the same time.

The next day while Jasper was off hiking, Frieda practiced. One: blink; two: blink-blink; three: blink-blink-blink. Again and again she tried. Over and over, until at last she cried out, "Oh, I can do it, I can do it. I actually can do it!"

That night when Jasper picked up his flashlight and blinked it one-two-three, Frieda answered with a blink-blink-blink. Jasper clapped his hands and shouted in surprise and joy. He was so loud, in fact, that Frieda became frightened and almost flew out of the tent.

For the rest of Jasper's stay at camp, Frieda flew to his tent at night and blinked one-two-three. Jasper answered with his flashlight, one-two-three.

After two weeks, Jasper left for home. Frieda returned to the tent site as usual, night after night, to blink three times, but there were no answering flashes. Sadly, she returned to her firefly friends. She tried to teach them about counting blinks, but they weren't interested.

A year passed. Once again Jasper appeared at the Scout camp. During his second hike in the woods, Jasper became separated from the others and that is how we found him at the beginning of this tale — sitting with a bowed head and feeling very lost and sad.

He knew that the Scoutmaster had told them if they ever got lost to stay where they were and not wander around. As darkness drew near, fireflies began to flicker all around him. Jasper was reminded of his little lightning bug friend of the year before and wished she were here now to keep him company.

Just then, out of the corner of his eye, Jasper saw a glow on his right shoulder. Blink-blink-blink! Blink-blink-blink! Jasper jumped to his feet, amazed. Was this his imagination? No, there it was again — blink-blink-blink. No mistake. It happened again and again. "My friend, my dear little friend," he shouted.

This was Frieda's woods and she knew the way back to camp. She flew in front of Jasper, then returned to his shoulder, until Jasper realized he was to follow her flickering light.

Frieda flew along, flashing blink-blink-blink, one-two-three. Jasper followed quickly until at last they came to the clearing and the Scout camp.

When the Scouts sat around the campfire that night, Jasper told about his experience with his firefly friend. But he had trouble convincing them, for Frieda had returned to her home in the woods and her firefly friends.

As time passed, Frieda taught her children to triple blink — blink-blink-blink, one-two-three. They taught their children, and so it went.

Who knows? Some night when you are camping near the woods in the midwest, watch closely as the fireflies flicker. You may see a bright, glowing blink-blink-blink.

NOTES TO PARENTS:

Has your child ever expressed interest in codes? Discuss the many ways messages can be sent: Morse code, body language, winks, nods, winces, folded arms, reversed words, letter substitution, numbers instead of letters, other languages...

Hepzebah Hopgrasser

Hepzebah was different! Mother Hopgrasser knew it immediately as she looked in amazement at her offspring. Hepzebah had the largest hind legs and feet she had ever seen! Even for a grasshopper. Father Hopgrasser blustered and fumed. "It certainly must come from your side of the family, the Jumpups," became his favorite saying.

Mother Hopgrasser smiled. "Of course. There was Grandfather Jumpup, who won the grand champion jumping competition. Could it be...?"

They could all see that it was a particularly plausible possibility that Hepzebah was not going to be just an ordinary grasshopper. Why, Hepzebah's very first venture out of her home was one very great leap! She landed far away from all of the others. Hepzebah's brothers and sisters, behind her, were taking small hops and nibbling grass as they went.

Mother Hopgrasser was very upset with Hepzebah for being so far from all of the others. It took Mother Hopgrasser five jumps to reach the place Hepzebah had reached with only one jump. Mother explained how it was not acceptable behavior for a little grasshopper to venture out on her own at such an early age. Hepzebah realized she had been wrong to worry her family so, and dutifully returned home.

The next day when it was time to go out, the family went together. Mother and Father Hopgrasser were very proud parents. It was all going quite well until old Mrs. Hop gawked at Hepzebah's feet. "Why look at that!" she said.

Everyone looked and pointed. "Well I never," "Imagine!" "They're so big," were remarks overheard by the family.

Poor Hepzebah felt embarrassed and tried to hide her big feet and long legs. Alas, it was useless. She just kept jumping higher and higher. At the end of the day, Hepzebah turned and, with one grand leap, landed right back at home. "I will stay inside forever!" she said.

Mother Hopgrasser felt sad, and decided that if Hepzebah wanted to hide her legs and feet, she would help. The next morning turned into a beautiful sunny day. Mother had worked all night and now was ready. She called Hepzebah and said, "Look what I have made for you!"

Hepzebah looked and saw, next to Mother, a daisy. This was not just a plain daisy, for the stem had been woven into a harness to hold Hepzebah's back legs.

Hepzebah wiggled into the harness and stood quietly while Mother secured it. Hepzebah looked wonderful, but when she tried to move, she could take only small steps. She crept from the home and nibbled grass, tender leaves, and clover as she went. Oh, she felt wonderful! She felt marvelous! Hepzebah felt great!

Oh, no! She felt so good she... just... had-to-jump.... And jump she did. Stem, daisy, and leaves all went flying, and Hepzebah was free! Higher and higher she jumped, and soon she felt grand!

Hepzebah leaped along happily until she remembered what she had been told: "I'm different." With that thought in mind, she fled back home as fast as she could jump.

Mother Hopgrasser thought and thought and thought about what to do. The next morning she was ready once again. When Hepzebah awoke, another surprise awaited. Mother had tied a stone onto Hepzebah's back legs, using interwoven dandelion stems. Oh, joy, joy! This would certainly keep Hepzebah from jumping too high.

Hepzebah went outside, this time seeking the tender leaves of the rhubarb plant. As she neared the rhubarb bed, dragging the stone behind her, she heard the sound of chomping and saw John Paul Jumpup, her cousin.

Everyone knew that John Paul had the biggest appetite in the neighborhood! Why, there would be nothing left for Hepzebah to eat! Hurry, Hepzebah, hurry! Forgetting the stone tied to her legs, she jumped. When Hepzebah jumped the second time, the stone broke free, sailed through the air, and landed next to John Paul, just missing hitting his head!

"Hey, Long Legs! You trying to kill me?" John Paul yelled.

Disappointed, Hepzebah returned home. *It was no use; it was no use at all,* she thought.

Mother Hopgrasser gave up trying to hold Hepzebah back from jumping. She tried again and again to build her child's confidence and assure her that everyone is different in some way or another. "That," Mother explained, "is what makes us interesting to others." Mother went on, "Why, look at Gwendolyn Hopper. Everyone in her family has a peculiar light green color!" She ended with, "My dear Hepzebah, you must be proud of who you are!"

Mother was right! Hepzebah was born to jump, and jump she would. She jumped once, twice, three times! She felt marvelous; she felt grand! Higher and higher, farther and farther went Hepzebah. Soon she was all alone and feeling free. She continued to jump about and leap happily.

Then it happened! After one tremendous leap, Hepzebah landed in a picnic basket. What glorious and delicious food Hepzebah found to nibble on. She ate and ate until at last she was full and so content that the only thing she could think of was sleep. She found a corner and, after curling up her big legs and feet, Hepzebah fell fast asleep.

She was wakened by an unfamiliar murmuring sound; she didn't know where she was. Everything around her seemed unfamiliar. She shook herself to remember, the picnic basket! It wouldn't be long before hands would reach into that basket and remove food. Oh no! Hepzebah was going to be discovered!

An exclamation of joy came from Audrey Meyers as she reached into the basket and very gently removed Hepzebah. "Just look what I have," exclaimed Audrey. "My very own pet!" The girl found a shoe box. "This is just the right size," she said. Audrey made a small bed of grass inside the box, adding a short twig for her pet to climb on, and then put in some tender leaves for food.   Hepzebah was lowered onto the nest. A box cover, complete with breathing holes, was placed over the top.

Hepzebah looked around forlornly. Where was the sunshine, so nice and warm? Where was the beautiful blue sky? Hepzebah tried to jump in every direction. Bang! Right into the side of the box. Bang! She hit the top of the box. After trying several times, Hepzebah gave up and sat on the nest of grass. Hepzebah's legs ached; she could not move them. She tried crawling around the box, but what she wanted to do was jump! Hepzebah crawled onto the little grass nest and cried and cried, until at last she fell asleep.

During the first few days that Audrey had her little pet, she remembered to take Hepzebah outside. Even though Hepzebah had to stay in the box, she enjoyed peeking through the air holes at the blue sky. Audrey picked new leaves for Hepzebah to eat. Still, she had a sad little grasshopper. What Hepzebah really wanted was to jump again! As summer wore on, Audrey became interested in other toys and games and forgot all about Hepzebah.

One day Audrey's mother found the box where Audrey had left it — on the back porch. She lifted the lid ever so slowly. This was just the chance Hepzebah was waiting for. With a mighty leap, Hepzebah broke free of the box and landed on the green lawn. Mrs. Meyers was so surprised she dropped the box and ran into the house. Hepzebah was free!

Hepzebah knew exactly where she was! It wasn't long before she leaped into the nest that was home. Mother and Father Hopgrasser were very happy to see her, for they had been worried. That night there was a family meeting. Now that she was home, what was to be done about Hepzebah's hopping habit?

Hepzebah sat in the corner listening. What was that Father just said? "Hepzebah's legs are an asset!" *What in the world is an asset? What did it mean?*

Hepzebah went over to Mother and asked, "What is an asset, Mother?"

"An asset," Mother explained, "is a thing of value. Something that you can be proud of!"

Something to be proud of! What could that be? "Oh, my legs and feet!" cried Hepzebah. How wonderful Hepzebah felt. How grand; how glorious. Why, Hepzebah could jump higher and farther than any other grasshopper, and Mother called it an *asset*!

The next day Father Hopgrasser showed Hepzebah some exercises to strengthen her legs. This would help her to jump even higher and farther. Hepzebah worked hard every day. Soon it was easy for her to do the exercises. Now when Hepzebah jumped, the friends and neighbors and, yes, even her brothers and sisters, cheered. "Look how high!" said one. "Look how far!" said another.

Mother and Father Hopgrasser were very pleased. "Now we are ready," Father said. "Now we are ready for the Olympics!" Hepzebah cheered.

Days passed and Hepzebah worked even harder than before. How wonderful to feel the wind whistle past as she jumped again and again.

At last the great day came. The family gathered together to cheer Hepzebah on. Down to the marshland they went, to the Marshfield Olympics.

Hepzebah had never jumped in front of a large crowd. *What if I fall? What if everyone laughs?*

Father Hopgrasser knew what was going through Hepzebah's mind. He gave Hepzebah good advice, "Just do as you did at home," he said, "what makes you feel wonderful, what you were meant to do... jump!"

By the time Hepzebah joined all the other contestants, she felt as if they were in her own back yard! With a big smile on her mouth, she took a very big breath, and Hepzebah leaped as never before!

The crowd cheered. Music broke forth from crickets, frogs, and birds. Never before had they seen a grasshopper jump so high and go so far! Hepzebah felt very proud as they hung the first place medal around her neck. Never since that wonderful day has there been a grasshopper that has beaten Hepzebah's records. But, someday... yes, someday!

NOTES TO PARENTS:

All children, at one time or another, feel as if they don't belong, that they are different. At the same time, they want to be acknowledged as unique. What a conundrum! Ask your child how they feel different from other kids. What is the thing they do or the appearance they have that gives them an outstanding, unique, special asset? And never accuse a child as being "like everybody else"!

Higher and Higher

Agatha nearly lost her grip as a brisk wind blew. She had climbed higher than any ant had ever climbed, for Agatha was on the very tip of the left ear of the General's Horse. The General Astride His Horse was a statue in the middle of the town park. Agatha's home was a large ant nest at the foot of the statue.

To begin at the beginning: Agatha began at first as an *egg*, laid by the queen ant in a small pretty room far down in the ant nest.

Agatha stayed there for several days. When she found she was getting much too big for the egg, she did what she must do... and that was to burst out. Now that Agatha had become what is called *larva*, the worker ants moved her to another room in the nest. At that point, Agatha looked small and white, and had no eyes or legs.

But she could eat! And eat she did. She ate and ate, and grew bigger and bigger, shedding her skin along the way.

"How bothersome," she thought. Every few days she had to shed her skin, which ants call *molting*. Agatha molted four more times as she grew. At last Agatha became a *pupa*, which is the next stage of an ant's growth. At that point the worker ants moved her to yet another room. Here Agatha spun a *cocoon* around her body and fell asleep. While she slept, great changes took place in her body. At last the great day came when her growing was complete.

The worker ants helped Agatha from her cocoon. There she stood in the little room, pale and weak, but determined to become a famous ant.

For one thing, Agatha had far better eyesight than the other ants, who could see only light and dark and some shapes. Agatha could see just about anything. Agatha knew she was a bit different and bound to do something great!

First Agatha explored the nest. She visited the room where she had lived as an egg. She viewed the nursery where the worker ants were tending the larvae. She looked into the storeroom where the food supply was kept, and the trash room for... what else? Trash! Why, she even peeked into the room of the queen ant, who was busily laying more eggs.

When Agatha learned all of the rooms by heart, it was time to explore the outside. She passed some worker ants who were building a new room. She passed worker ants who were cleaning out the old rooms. As she approached the entrance of the nest, she passed worker ants busily scurrying in and out bringing food for the queen and the young ants.

Agatha crept to the entrance and peered over the edge. Before her she saw a wooded area. Agatha turned around slowly and viewed trees, park benches, a picnic table, a playground, flowers, bushes, and grass. Then Agatha turned around and looked up... and up... and... up. Far above her loomed the biggest statue in the town. It was the General, sitting on his horse. The General looked very proud!

In the early morning, Agatha slowly crawled forward from the nest. She felt around with her antennae. *First things first*, she thought as she cleaned her antennae with the bristles on her front legs. She knew her antennae were very important to her body; without them she would be helpless.

Agatha scrambled through the grass. She smelled food. She continued until she crawled under a picnic table and there, sure enough, was a large crumb of bread that the robins had overlooked. The crumb was twice as big as Agatha, but she was strong. She dragged, carried, pushed, and shoved the crumb to the entrance of the nest and there, with the help of other workers, dragged it to the food storage room. It was good fun and great exercise to scamper out again and again to find crumbs and other food to bring back to the nest.

Remember though, Agatha was not an average ant. She had big ideas of doing great things.

One morning as she emerged from the nest, instead of going through the grass as the others did, Agatha climbed to the top of the hoof of the horse statue. She looked all around. She could see all of the worker ants gathering food. *I wonder what more I could see if I was at the top of the leg?*

From where Agatha was at the bottom looking up, it was a long way to climb. Agatha knew her feet had those special claws for climbing and clinging, as all ants have, so up she went.

When she arrived at the top of the horse's leg, she stopped and looked around. Now she could see the entire playground, the swings, teeter-totter, slippery slide, merry-go-round, and all of the children playing. *If I can see this good from here*, she thought, *how much better could I see from the top of the horse's head?* With a smile on her face and determination in her heart, up she climbed.

When she reached the top of the horse's head, she looked around and found just the right spot to stay. It was under the left ear of the horse where she could look all around for as long as she wanted to.

For the rest of the day that is just what she did. She saw flowers and trees, people walking and playing ball, and the lovely children playing in the playground. What a wonderful afternoon!

As the day wore on, Agatha became hungry and it was getting dark. Agatha climbed down to the ant nest, ate supper, and went to sleep.

The next day, because she remembered how hungry she had been the day before, Agatha made a trip to the picnic table. She found a crumb of chocolate cake just the right size and carried it up to her favorite place at the base of the left ear of the horse statue.

All day she watched people jogging, walking, riding bicycles, and picnicking in the park. She especially enjoyed watching the children on the playground. That night just before she fell asleep, she had an idea!

The very next day when she reached the entrance to the nest, instead of climbing to her favorite spot, she went over to the playground. She crawled first to the top of the slippery slide. She knew what it was for, because she had watched the children slide down. Putting her tummy flat against the slide and spreading her six legs out to her sides, away she went. Swish! Plop! Right down to the ground. This may have been all right for children, but for a tiny ant it was quite an adventure and quite a hard bump. Not a thing Agatha thought she wanted to do again.

Therefore, she went over to the teeter-totter and climbed onto the board and up to the highest side. It wasn't long before two children ran to the teeter-totter and climbed on. Down went the side with Agatha, then up in the air. Then down, then up, then down with a hard thump that sent Agatha bouncing off onto the ground. *Well, that certainly was fun*, thought Agatha.

With that, she went right over to the merry-go-round. There were no children on it, but Agatha crawled on anyway. One minute hadn't passed before three children threw themselves onto the merry-go-round and a fourth child pushed it around faster and faster. Whee! What fun! Oh my, Agatha felt a bit dizzy. Oh, my, Agatha felt very, very dizzy. She wouldn't be able to hold on much longer! At the very first chance, when the merry-go-round slowed down, Agatha jumped off. She landed on the shoe of one of the children who was going to the swings.

I might as well go along, thought Agatha. Up and down, back and forth went the swing. This was one ride Agatha liked. She didn't feel dizzy. She didn't get thumped. She didn't get bumped. She had fun!

That night when Agatha crawled into bed, she was very tired, and also very very happy!

Days and days passed. Each day Agatha went to the horse's ear. She thought and thought about what she could do that no other ant had ever done. *I'm higher than any ant has ever climbed. Or am I?* thought Agatha. She looked around. Her eyes fell upon a tall flagpole. She looked again, up and up to the very tip-top. *That's it*, she thought, *that's it! I will climb to the very tip top of the flagpole*!

The very next morning she started her journey. She carried a large crumb of chocolate cake, for it was her favorite food. By suppertime, she had reached the bottom of the flagpole where she nibbled on her crumb of chocolate cake and went to sleep.

The next day Agatha awoke very early. She finished her cake and cleaned her antennae with her legs. Then she took a deep breath and began her trip to the top of the flagpole.

Up and up she climbed. She stopped now and then to rest and explore with her antennae. She continued up and up and up. Soon when she stopped she could see the tops of the trees. Up and up, higher and higher, she went, where the wind was much stronger. *Hang on, Agatha*, she encouraged herself; *hang on*!

She was almost at the top. One last rest stop, then up she went. The pole swayed in the breeze. Agatha grasped the top with all of her claws and looked around.

The view was beautiful. The sky was blue. She could see buildings, cars driving up and down the street, people walking along streets, looking as tiny as ants as they entered and left buildings. The birds flew right past her. Oh, she felt glorious!

This time Agatha was certain. No other ant had ever been this high! Or was there something she didn't know about?

NOTES TO PARENTS:

Get an idea of your child's feelings about daring, climbing, high places, competition, trying. If the child expresses fears, discuss them. Some fear heights or the dark or trying something new or losing... or winning. You may be surprised.

Dancing Leaves

On this beautiful day, the daffodils and tulips already had opened their pretty faces to the sun. Earlier, the rain had added a shiny newness to everything outside. The sky took on a fresh warm blue hue with soft fluffy clouds here and there.

This was the particular day that Winifred Willowleaf first poked her head out from a bud. Her home was on the topmost branch of a drooping Weeping Willow tree. The tree stood on the banks of a rippling stream that faced the edge of the woods.

Winifred had felt the light rain that morning and now she felt the sun's warm rays. All of the warmth caused Winifred to break free of her budding state and spread out to her full slender length. How good it felt to be out in the fresh air, to feel the wind's soft touch that sent the branches around her dipping and swaying.

Winifred's first attempts at dancing and swaying were graceful to see. Mother Willow was proud of all her thousands of gracefully rippling willow leaves.

Close by the willow tree grew a majestic poplar tree, whose height was greater than the willow by at least a foot. Polly Poplar lived on one of the uppermost branches.

Polly noticed Winifred first, and waved her lovely silver green body in a friendly way. Winifred responded by giving her branch a big dip as she swayed, and she waved back. In this manner, they greeted each other every day.

One morning the sun did not greet Winifred as usual. Instead, gray clouds filled the sky. Suddenly a brilliant flash of lightning was followed by a loud clap of thunder. Winifred shook. *My goodness*! she thought. *What is going on?*

The wind blew stronger and stronger, whipping poor Winifred this way and that. It was all she could do to hang onto her branch. She glanced over at Polly Poplar during one flash of lightning and saw Polly holding on as well as she could. Winifred could see only Polly's silver back and not her friendly green top at all. *Oh dear, oh dear, what could happen next?* wondered Winifred.

In a short time, Polly and Winifred found out exactly what happened next. Large drops of water began to fall from the sky. Soon Winifred was drenching wet. She continued to dip and sway faster and faster. She certainly wasn't having as much fun as she did when the sun was shining.

Before long, Winifred's first rainstorm was over and the sun again shone down on Winifred Willowleaf. As she dried off, she began to sway and dance again. This was only the first of many storms to come along that summer.

As much as Winifred liked to dance and sway, she knew her first duty as a good leaf was to feed the mother tree. She took the water as it was sent up from the tree roots and, with the help of the sunshine, turned it into food for the tree. She was kind of a food factory that changed the water into sugar for the tree's food. Winifred hurried through her duties each day so she would have plenty of time to enjoy her dancing.

One day Winifred noticed Polly Poplar waving in a different direction. Winifred turned to see that Polly was waving at a pretty dark green, curly maple leaf, whose name she discovered was Malinda Mapleleaf.

What fun the three leaves had that summer, bowing and swaying, sometimes together and sometimes in opposite directions. Winifred liked to show the others how low her branch could dip, far lower than any of the other trees.

As summer changed to autumn, the days became shorter and shorter. The nights became cooler. One afternoon, Winifred felt something cold fall upon her, fallen from the sky. Looking up she saw, sure enough, millions and millions of tiny snowflakes coming down. At first she had great fun dodging the flakes. She dodged this way and that, but soon there were too many. Winifred grew tired and let the snowflakes cover her as they were quickly covering all the millions of other leaves. This caused the branches of all the trees to dip alarmingly low. The next morning just as Winifred thought her branch would break, the sun came out and melted all of the snow. What a relief!

Winifred was using her food factory less and less, causing her to lose her green color. This was because she no longer was producing *chlorophyll*, the substance that made her color green. Instead, Winifred's color was turning yellow. She glanced over at Polly, whose color also had turned a bright brilliant yellow.

Together they waved at Malinda Mapleleaf who had turned a gorgeous bright orange with yellow tips. *She certainly is a beauty*, thought Winifred.

Now that Winifred Willowleaf was no longer needed to make food for the tree, she spent each day dancing and swaying. Before long she realized that something was happening. A layer of cork was growing over her *petiole*, that part of her that held her to the branch. This shut off Winifred completely from her branch.

So it was that on one cool autumn day, just as the wind began to blow briskly across the land, Winifred lost her hold on the branch and floated gracefully to the ground.

When she landed, she looked up, and who should be gliding down towards her but Polly Poplar. And next to Polly was Malinda Mapleleaf. They both floated majestically until they reached Winifred's side.

There on the ground lay the three leaves, each a beautiful color. They glanced around and saw millions of other leaves just like them, all with wonderful colors. Each of them had fallen from their branches to the ground.

The wind blew once more and sent the three leaves dancing across the brown fields. Winifred noticed that some of her leaf friends had fallen into a rippling stream and were swirling around as the water carried them downstream.

The three leaves found a small space at the base of a large oak tree and huddled together.

That is where they were discovered by a boy of nine, named Joshua. Joshua, a Cub Scout, was making a display of his leaf collection. He needed just three more leaves to complete it, and here they were, right at his feet.

Joshua bent down and carefully picked up Winifred, Polly, and Malinda. He carried them to his house where he gently smoothed out each leaf as flat as he could so that all of their beautiful colors showed. Then he placed a drop of glue on each one and pressed them onto a large board. Under each one he printed the name of their family tree.

Under Winifred he printed "Willowleaf". Under Polly he wrote "Poplar". Under Malinda he put "Mapleleaf". Winifred was amazed that he knew their family names.

All three leaves were very proud to be part of Joshua's collection. They stayed just as bright and glorious as they could that night as Joshua showed his collection to all the other Scouts. Believe it or not, there on the corner of Joshua's display the beautiful leaves saw the blue ribbon — meaning his collection was the best.

NOTES TO PARENTS:

Has your child started a collection of anything? Talk about some collection ideas: bottle caps, pictures of something, comic strips, books, flowers, weeds, action figures, turtles (real and otherwise), handprints...

Tulympia

(A Poem For the Young At Heart)

Here I lay atop my pillow
Which is placed upon my
bed,
That has strawberries
embroidered
Where I set my weary head.
My forest sheets enfold me
As I snuggle further down,
Pull my flowered quilt up o'er me
As I enter Comfortown.

* * *

Comfortown is in Tulympia,
A country oh so grand;
There reside so many people
Living throughout all the land.

In the castle lives King Tulip
With Petalia, his queen.
Then there's Princess Tulipetta
And the Wise Man Florentine.

The sun shone through the fabric,
Made it real as real can be,
King Tulip stated to the Queen,
"Queen Petalia," said he,
"I am concerned, concerned am I
Our Princess is so sad.
See how her head is drooping,
With her color looking bad."

"We must help our dear sweet princess,"
Queen Petulia answered him.
"Take her walking in the forest,
Let her picnic in the glen.
Now come here and eat the meal
That I have prepared for thee.
There's strawberry bread with strawberry jam
And a cup of strawberry tea."

Strawberries are the diet
Of Comfortown, you know.
They eat them morning, noon, and night,
For a treat, it's strawberry snow
Which is not unlike ice cream,
For it's flavorful and cold.
Plus, a diet of plain strawberries
Is wonderful, I'm told.

With the meal completed,
They set to the task at hand.
They must help the princess see herself
As the fairest in the land.
They must help the princess laugh again,
To romp and play and dance.
They must help her now, to love herself,
Yes, they would take the chance.

They sought out Wise Man Florentine
With his royal purple hue.

What is the magic answer?
What is the magic brew?
"Florentine," the grand king thundered,
"Tell us please, our good dear friend,
How can we help the princess?
To us, a message send."

Florentine spread wide his arms
And lifted high his head.
"Listen well, my king and queen,
Harken when 'tis said,"
He began in a grumbly voice
Like thunder far away.
As he progressed throughout his tale
His body began to sway.

"Down in the deep dark recesses,
Down in the valley cold,
Lies Bedfootville, a dark dank place,
With its King Amaranth, bold.

No meaner king alive is there,
More wicked is Queen Perslane,
And troublesome Prince Nettle
Will cause problems, it is plain.

"Plus on the edge of town there is
A sorcerer of kind.
It is the evil Solanum
Whose spells of magic bind.
You must find an agile body
Who can climb and run and hide,
Who can enter murky countrytown
Where trouble does abide.

"For past the home of Solanum,
Lies a field of stickseed weed
With thistle, sorrel, and knotgrass
Whose manners you must heed.
Then come you to a mountain
And at the very base
Must be dug a hole two feet deep
'Neath the tree with the yellow face.

"Avoid a troll named Parsnip;

Avoid his harmful waste.

Grasp the colored stone from the hollow well

And bring it back, post haste!

For the stone has magic powers

That come down from above.

It can help our dear sweet princess

Find herself; then she can love."

There were just two, they both agreed,

To do the job with speed,

With strength, agility, and craft,

Which is their very need.

Susan and Shasta Daisy

Were held in high esteem.

"They'll help us, I know they will,"

Said Petulia, the queen.

The twins ran to the castle.

What would their good king say?

They entered into his presence
And nodded their heads, "Good day."
All was explained in detail
And, when the tale was through,
They set out on their journey.
It was dangerous, they knew.

Slowly through the forest,
A slip past Kneesbent Mound,
Down toward the dark and dreary place
Where the treasures could be found.
Castle Footshigh loomed ahead.
Yes, there were the king and queen.
How wicked they looked, how evil.
The twins hoped they'd not be seen.

Prince Nettle was there at his parents' side.
Did he see them? He looked their way.
No, he was picking on Little Flower
That came over just to play.
As they watched, Little Flower jumped away
And landed close, near by

Where the Daisys both were hiding,
And the Flower began to cry.

"We will save you," stated Shasta
As he wiped away a tear.
And the little violet answered,
"Thank you, I will not fear."
So he hid her 'neath the willow tree,
Drew her leaves around her head.
And you still find her hiding there,
In her little violet bed.

The twins continued on their jaunt.
"I'm hungry," Susan said.
So they sat and filled their tummies
With dried strawberries and bread.
When they were done, they slipped away
Then came Solanum's cave.
Quietly, they made their way,
Worrisome, but brave.

Near the entrance, at the door,
Susan spied a spade.
"We'll need that when we get there,
If a hole is to be made."
Shasta knew that this was true
As silently they crept.
Then, they heard Solanum snoring
And they knew Solanum slept.

They tied the spade to Shasta's back
With a piece of strawberry twine.
Then lowered themselves so carefully
Down a steep, slipp'ry incline.
Here was the stickweed pasture
Which went on a long, long ways.
They both had brought sticks
To push them back
As they started through the maze.

It was difficult to make their way.
The thistles grabbed and stung.
They pushed along this way and that,

Their bats heartily swung.

At last they made it to the edge

And jumped clear; they were free!

They rested 'side a bubbling brook

And drank strawberry tea.

The Footboard Mountain loomed high above.

They were ready to find the place

To dig the hole and find the stone

'Neath the tree with the yellow face.

They searched this way and they searched that,

But nothing did they find

Til they spied, off to the left,

Some honeysuckle vine.

"See how it wrapped around that trunk

And formed a face – 'tis true.

Yes, this was the tree with the yellow face,"

And they knew just what to do.

They dug a hole just two feet deep

As Florentine had bade.

The twins were so excited

As they soon threw down the spade.

While lying flat, they reached deep inside.

"I've got it, I've got it, I do!"

Shasta cried as he lifted the stone up above,

"It's beautiful, shiny as new."

They tied a stone secure to his waist

And refilled the hole so fast,

Left the spade for Solanum to find.

Well, they could go home at last!

But alas and alack, 'twas not to be.

When only a few steps they'd taken.

The two of them found they were held fast

And felt as if all was forsaken.

'Twas Parsnip the troll who held them tight.

"You'll not get away from me now."

Then Susan said, "If we wanted to go,

Couldn't you please tell us how?"

Parsnip laughed at her courage, and said,

"There's only one way you'll be freed,

I know you can't." He grinned cruel and wide.

"Show me proof you've done a good deed."

Time passed as they pondered and thought.
"I know what we've done," Shasta said,
"We saved little Violet and hid her away,
But we have no proof, for we fled."

Yes, they'd saved Violet, of that they were sure.
But it's no proof; only they knew.
Then Susan gasped, her eyes opened wide.
As she saw the answer so true!
"Look!" Susan cried, "where you wiped a tear
With your petal so soft, it's a stain!
Yes, it's left a spot, right there near the end.
We've done a good deed, it is plain."

Parsnip sputtered and fumed when he saw the
place,
'Twas a stain that looked like a tear.
Well, that was the proof they'd done a good
deed.
"I'll have to let you go, I fear."
With silence and speed they raced toward home
And arrived at the castle in days.

They found Florentine and gave him the stone.

He rewarded them with grateful praise.

Florentine found the princess and stood at her
side,

Placed the stone carefully in her hand.

"Look way deep, to its inner core,

You'll see its colors so grand.

Then find its deepest secret,

Find its beauty and grandeur too.

Soon you will have the answer

To discover the inner you."

She rubbed the stone's smoothness, felt all its
contours.

She saw oceans, clouds, flowers and trees;

She saw birds in flight and fishes that swim.

Then she knew as she saw all of these.

This stone had come from the mountain,

But that did not mean it was less.

It still had the mountainous beauty inside;

It still was able to impress!

So, I'm not just a shell; I'm not empty inside;
I have beauty and strength; I am whole!
For just as the mountain was still in the stone,
My creator is still in my soul!
So then the princess was happy,
Free to laugh and dance and sing.
And all those around her joined in the fun,
Even the queen and the king.

"What I learned was in my heart;
I'm really somebody.
No rock in my hand," said the princess,
"Can change that fact for me.
I can love me as I am.
I'm important, I'm my friend;
I'm special, I'm beloved;
I'll be loyal to the end."

* * *

I awake from my dream with a yawn and a
stretch
And open my eyes to the sun,
Knowing I will return to Tulympia,
The adventures have just begun.
Like Tulipetta, I see who I am!
I'm important, just like she said.
I am me; I am loved; I am happy and glad.
So, with that thought, I jump out of bed.

NOTES TO PARENTS:

Ask your child to write a short poem — four to a
dozen lines. Select a subject. Write a poem of
your own on the same subject. Share. If your
child is unable to write, ask for a verbal poem.
And love every offered poem!

V-E-N-T-I-

This is the story of Venti the Mouse
Who was born in a rowboat and
not in a house.
Mother Mouse was named Wella;
Her family were many.
There was Great Great Aunt Jo
And fun Uncle Lenny.

Wella stayed busy, like all mother mice,
Giving names to her children; she wanted them
nice.
She wanted to do as her mother, you see,
Who had named all her children with A to Z.
She had many young ones; she'd used A and B.
My goodness, she thought, *I'm way down to V.*

There is Ali and Berry, Casey and Darrell,

Earl and Fanny, Gussie and Harrell.
Then came Inez and Jello (took that off a box),
Then Kelly and Lemmy and Newton and Ox.
He's always the biggest, that Ox, where was I?
Oh yes, Pansy, Quinella, Rusty and Si.

Tuffy, Ulysses, now V, think, think, think;
And it came to her then, quick as a wink.
There was before her, a sign somewhat torn.
'Twas the name "The ADVENTURE,"
That weather had worn.
It had washed away "AD," part of "U" and "RE."
What was left was just "VENTI,"
A fine name thought she.

So Venti grew up living down by Lake Drothers,
Eating berries and playing with sisters and
brothers.
One night came a windstorm. Oh my goodness
sake!
It gusted, it blustered them into the lake!

They were all in the boat as it dashed on the water;
They went this way and that way, all tish and a totter.

The family was seasick; my, what was their fate?
But, not our dear Venti; she thought it was great!
The boat was soon found on the opposite shore
And brought back home safely. "We'll travel no more!"
Said Father and Mother Mouse, still greatly shook.
"We'll get our adventures from reading a book."

Alas and alack, this was not meant to be,
For the owners went fishing; the mice could not flee.
"Stay quiet," said Mother. "Stay right where you are."
Venti couldn't just sit there; she ventured afar.

She went, oh so quietly, up to the top
Where she peeked, oh so carefully, humans to
spot.
There were just two, one rowing, one fishing.
"I wish I could join them," Venti was wishing.
She'd... creep... up... closer... to see how it's done.
Slow wasn't her speed, for she'd rather run.

"I'll just sit on this box; now I see a lot."
Then the boat gave a lurch and she fell out —
ker-plop!
Venti rolled up and over, then over and up,
And got to her feet near a white coffee cup.
The human screamed, "Yeeow!" and made such
a flurry,
Venti headed for home in a huff and a hurry.

She'd a tear in her eye as she looked back so
sadly.
She just wanted to fish and she wanted it badly.

When they got back to shore, Venti sat just a-
wishing,
"There must be a way that I can go fishing."
She asked all her friend mice, and her family
clan
To help her think up a splendiferous plan.

Earl found a toy boat a child had left lying.
Ali found some string without even trying.
Mother found some cloth a few inches wide,
And some milkweed-pod cotton for stuffing
inside.
She stitched and she sewed; she cut and she
tore;
She made a life jacket for Venti. Wait, there's
more.

Father Mouse found a toothpick, just the right
size,
And a couple old eyelets for making the guides
To put the white string in. Then oh, such a deal!
He found he had made her a rod and a reel.

To top it all off, Fanny made her a hat
Just like sailors wear. Well, just think of that!

So now you find Venti on Friday or Sunday,
Tuesday or Thursday, or Wednesday or Monday,
Or any nice day that the humans go fishing,
Venti goes too, just as she was a-wishing.
She's behind the big rowboat, with cord tied so
tight,
Sitting and waiting for her own fish to bite.

And Mother says soon we'll be taking a look
At Winky, Xavier, Yolanda and Zook.

NOTES TO PARENTS:

The youngest may catch on to the alphabet
thing. How many fruits can you name with
different beginning letters? Name a flower for
each of the letters in your name. Think of an
animal for each letter in the alphabet. Name the
letters that rhyme with "Me"!

The Choice Chirping of Clavier Cricket

It was a happy, beautiful spring day when the little crickets emerged from the eggs that Mother Cricket had laid last autumn.

Clavier was the very last of the little crickets to emerge. Of course the little cricket was not named Clavier at that time. No, it wasn't until Mother Cricket heard the beautiful sounds made by the little cricket that she found the name of Clavier, which is also the name of a stringed instrument.

Father Cricket stood Clavier in line with all of the other little crickets. "This is the sound to be made by crickets," he said as Father chirped his cricket chirrup. All down the line the little crickets imitated Father's chirrup. Although some were not as good as others. When it was Clavier's turn, the other crickets listened in amazement. For, trying as hard as a little cricket could manage, Clavier could not make the chirrup sound the way that Father Cricket had. What came out of Clavier's scraper and file was a beautiful melody. This sound dismayed Father Cricket, for he thought it was a good cricket's duty to herald summer with a correct sounding chirrup.

Mother Cricket, however, was delighted. She listened for hours as Clavier played away.

"What high notes! What low tones," she crooned. "What a blessing on the ear."

Clavier's nest was situated just off the patio and to the left of the house where the Westchesters lived. Clavier, an outside cricket, had an amazing experience one day. As Mother Westchester gathered the sheets and towels from the clothesline, Clavier was caught up in the laundry basket and taken into the house.

"What a beautiful, large nest this is," thought Clavier. For all homes are nests to crickets.

Clavier explored every inch of the family room — the family room being where Clavier landed when jumping out of the laundry basket. Clavier found the perfect place to stay —inside the back of the Westchesters' stereo speaker.

That night just as the sun sank and while there was still a pink glow in the western sky, Mother Westchester turned on the stereo. Now, Mother Westchester was particularly fond of violin music and chose a Viennese Waltz. Clavier listened a long time. As the music played on, Clavier couldn't help but join in. When the violins reached the high notes, so did Clavier. When the violas reached the low notes, so did Clavier. So in tune was Clavier that Mother Westchester was not even aware of the extra sound. When the record was done and the stereo turned off, Clavier continued with great happiness, to produce the violin sounds.

Mother Westchester was extremely confused. She checked the stereo twice to make sure that it was turned off. "Where could the sounds be coming from?" she asked. She listened intently and then moved toward the speaker. She turned the speaker around slowly and saw Clavier, who was still making the sounds that gave such pleasure. Mother Westchester picked up Clavier carefully and called for the family to come and see what she had found. Clavier was so frightened that the sound stopped.

Father Westchester had read somewhere that in Japan people made little wooden cages for singing crickets. It was believed by these people that the cricket brought good fortune to the house. With this in mind, Father Westchester made a little wooden cage for Clavier.

As Clavier was so well cared for — with a good supply of grain to eat, and a nice warm nest to sleep in — the cricket again began making the beautiful sounds. At first it was just with the stereo. Later, Clavier made the sounds even when the stereo was not playing.

Now, Clavier wished to be the very best at making the beautiful sounds. Clavier also knew that the only way this could come about was to practice and practice. So, practice Clavier did, sometimes far into the night the Westchester family could hear Clavier practicing. Clavier was getting better — and better — and better!

One night after one of the Westchester children had given Clavier grain, the top of the cage was left open. Now we all know that little crickets, besides making chirrup sounds, have an enormous curiosity. So Clavier jumped — and jumped — and jumped — and finally with one big jump — Clavier landed outside the cage and onto the family room floor.

Clavier hopped underneath the coffee table and, thinking it to be a safe place, began to make the lovely sounds. This was just too much for the Westchester's dog Patches, who happened to be taking an afternoon nap in the very same room. Patches immediately began to investigate. Patches went right up to Clavier and sniffed and sniffed. Clavier was very frightened by all of this attention and became very — very quiet. Patches reached out a paw and gave Clavier a nudge. Well, this was just too much for Clavier, who gave a little hop. Patches, believing this to be a delightful game, sniffed once again, gave a playful nudge, and this time added a happy bark! This was definitely too much! Clavier gave a big hop this time and found the stereo speaker close by and scurried in.

This action aroused Patches to a greater fury and Patches responded with many loud barks. Mother Westchester came running to see what all of the noise was about. After quieting Patches, who was then put outside, Mother discovered poor little Clavier shaken and huddled in the corner of the speaker. She quickly and carefully placed Clavier back into the little cage.

A few days later Mother Westchester, knowing how delighted Clavier was with music, decided to take Clavier along when they went to the symphony.

It was wonderful. Clavier could hardly stay quiet during the music. After the symphony was over, Mother and Father Westchester, with Clavier in the cage, went backstage. When they found the conductor, they told of their unusual and very talented cricket.

The conductor wanted to hear for himself. He picked up a violin and began to play. Clavier could not stay quiet any longer. As the violin music grew louder, Clavier joined in. What a marvelous duet it was. How amazed the conductor became at the clear tones that Clavier made.

"I will write a symphony just for our little friend," promised the conductor. And that is just what was done.

On the evening the orchestra was to play "The Little Cricket", everyone was very excited.

The Westchester family put on their very finest clothes. With Clavier in the cage, the family drove to the auditorium where the orchestra was to play. When they arrived, Mother Westchester walked right up to the front of the room and placed the cage on the stage right next to the conductor.

The hall grew quiet as the first strains of the music were played. Then as the music swelled, Clavier joined in. It was grand; it was glorious; Clavier was very happy.

Back in the very farthest and darkest corner of the auditorium huddled a small group together. They were Mother and Father Cricket with their whole family. How they chirped when the music stopped. They were all very — very — very — proud!

NOTES TO PARENTS:

Ask your child what they think would make you proud. What would make them proud? Describe the difference between "pride" and "egotism".

Elizabeth

Scurry, scurry, faster,
faster ran the little
earwig. The lizard chasing her snapped its jaws.
"Must get away," thought the little bug.

Just then she saw a log that had fallen
during the last night's rain, a very good place to
hide. She quickly darted under the bark of the
log and wedged herself into a slim space.

"Whew! That was close!" she thought. The
little earwig settled down to sleep, for it was
getting light out. You see, earwigs are
nocturnal; that means they are livelier during
the night and rest up during the daylight hours.

About that time a little girl named Holly
was tramping through the woods with her
mother and a few classmates. Her class had
been studying insects this month and Holly had

memorized many of the appearances and names of the bugs. In fact, they had started an insect study club. They called themselves the "Bug Club".

The children were deep in the woods when they saw a fallen log. "Just the place for insects to hide," shouted Holly. She saw the little earwig and called to her friends, "Oh, look! What a beautiful earwig."

There sat the little bug — a beautiful reddish brown earwig trying very hard to be invisible. "I've never seen a more beautiful insect," said Holly. "Mother, may I take her home? Please? I'll make a cozy nest for her and we'll play together and have lots of fun!"

Holly knew it was a little girl earwig, for the girls have straight forceps-like pincers while the males have curved pincers. "I'll name her Elizabeth," said Holly. "We'll have a fun time!"

Holly carried Elizabeth safely in her pocket for the rest of the hike. Elizabeth Earwig was happy just to rest and be carried.

When they arrived at Holly's home, the girl quickly called "Daddy, Daddy. Look what I have!"

Her dad admired Elizabeth. "She's beautiful. What a fine specimen of an earwig," he said. Together Holly and her dad hunted for a small box to make a home for Elizabeth. Holly found a small empty cereal box. She cut a flap on the top and bent it back, then placed a folded handkerchief inside, along with a few wood chips and a few pieces of cereal. She made a perfect home for her pet.

Holly taught Elizabeth to play hide-and-seek. Every morning when the little earwig came home from being with her friends, she hid in a different place. Holly hunted and hunted until she found Elizabeth.

Mother had saved a few paper towel rolls and gave them to Holly. They taped them together to make a long tube. "Look Elizabeth," said Holly. "We've made you a fun tunnel." Holly placed the bug at one end of the tunnel and went to the other end to call her name. After Elizabeth learned to run through the tunnel, what fun they had.

One day Father called the family together. He told them he had a problem. He needed to move a few electric wires from the back of the house to the front. To do the job, he had bought a two-inch PVC pipe to run the width of the house. The problem was how to get the wires through the tube?

"I know," said Holly. "Elizabeth and I will help." The little earwig had grown to one-and-a-half inches and was getting stronger each day.

Father thought a moment before he said, "There's no way a little bug can pull those big wires. I could tie some cord to the wires, but it still would be too big. Then I could tie some string to the cord. Maybe just maybe…"

Mother spoke up, lifting a spool of red thread from her sewing basket. "This is thin enough. Can you use it?"

"That's exactly what I need!" said Father.

He measured the thread to match the length of the tube and tied one end onto the string, making a loop on the other end.

'Yes! Yes!" shouted Holly. "Elizabeth can pull that!"

She told Elizabeth what she needed to do, slipped the loop of thread over the earwig's pincer and said, "Now run to the other side, just like your fun tunnel." Elizabeth started out, slowly at first, then faster.

She became apprehensive. Maybe there are lizards in the tube! But, she knew that she could squirt a foul-smelling yellow liquid from her scent glands if she needed to protect herself.

She scurried on, feeling her way along the tunnel.

Soon she caught sight of the light at the end. Yes, she heard Holly calling her name. When the little earwig arrived at the end of the tube tunnel, Holly lifted the little bug out, slipped the loop from around her and handed the thread to her Dad.

Dad pulled oh-so-gently until the string came out. Then he tugged on the string until the cord got free. When he dragged the cord through the tube, the wires appeared. "Hurrah! We did it," shouted Dad. "Three cheers for Elizabeth!" Both Holly and Elizabeth felt very proud!

That's not quite the end of the story. Time for play was cut short as Holly grew older. Then came the day the little earwig was put back on the log in the forest where she found her friends just under the bark.

Today if you are in the forest and look under the bark of a log, you may just maybe find some reddish-brown earwigs. Chances are they are Elizabeth's relatives!

NOTES TO PARENTS:

Has your child ever solved a problem by figuring a special way to do it? Ask, "How would you solve Holly's dad's problem if you didn't have an educated earwig?

Oliver Ogden Oglethorpe!

(An Adventurous Dung Beetle)

There's really nothing wrong with the name Oliver Ogden Oglethorpe The Third. It was his grandfather's name, his father's name, and now his. Everyone called him Oogie, obviously from his initials. That's all right with him. He's just "Oogie".

But that became the problem!

All day long, from sun-up to sun-down, Oogie rolls dung (another name for manure). Starting when he was small, he rolled and patted, rolled and patted, making his ball bigger and bigger. When it got too big to handle, Oogie rolled it over to mix with the others. Then he started another one. Roll — pat — roll — pat.

Oh don't think he's bored. Oogie loves what he does. He knows he's helping the environment. But that's not enough. Oogie wants to be famous and he wants everyone to know his real name.

He dreams of hearing them say, "There goes Oliver Ogden Oglethorpe the Third! Isn't he great, wonderful, glorious, stupendous?"

Mother's voice broke into his thoughts, "Oogie, time for bed," she called.

And so it went for a time. But not for long. Oogie came up with an idea! He'd go on an adventure.

One dark night, Oogie slid out of bed, put his favorite hat on his head, rolled up his bed, slung it over his back and walked out of the nest. Using the Milky Way to guide him, he began an adventure! (Curious nature fact: dung beetles are currently the only known insect to navigate using the Milky Way!)

Oogie walked down the lane, across the field, toward the lights of the Big Metropolis...

city, that is... at least big for a small dung beetle.

He found his way to an abandoned motel. Looking around, he found a small mouse hole, empty of mice, and a fine place to put his bed roll. So spreading it out, he lay down and fell fast asleep.

When he awoke, he thought for a minute that he was home. He looked around for the dung pile and all his friends, but no, he was alone, on an adventure!

First things first. He nibbled the bit of dung he had stuck under his left wing. And he drank a little water from a puddle just outside his new home. (Curious nature fact: dung beetles get their nourishment from eating dung!)

When he had finished, he started out to walk. He walked on and on. Because he was among many people, he had to avoid being stepped on.

He saw children playing and went to join them. The smallest girl was named Beth. She had a picnic basket on her arm, which she set down on the porch.

Beth's father, Ed, was the owner of a fertilizer factory on the edge of town. Within the factory was an enormous reservoir of water held back by an earthen dam. This was the source of power for lights and machinery in the factory.

As a very curious and adventuresome dung beetle, Oogie climbed into Beth's basket on the porch. Oh, the smells were wonderful, which made him hungry. When he felt the basket as she picked it up, he settled down for a ride. The children soon reached their destination on the edge of town, in the shadow of Beth's father's factory. Were they on a picnic? This was a gloriously beautiful day! Until they heard Beth's father, Ed, calling to them, "Run, the dam is going to break up!"

The children quickly gathered up their things and ran. Ed picked up some of the baskets, including the one with Oogie inside. "I can fill some of the holes in the dam with this straw," he explained.

As Ed ran out to warn the family, he had knocked over some sacks of fertilizer, which spilled out onto the floor.

Oogie peeked out and saw the dam with all the little holes beginning to appear. Looking down, he saw the fertilizer on the floor. Instinct took over; he knew what he must do. Jumping out of the basket onto the floor, he started gathering the fertilizer: rolling, patting, rolling, patting.

"Look what this little dung beetle is doing," shouted Ed. Bending down he picked up the little bundle Oogie had made and plugged up one of the holes in the dam. It worked! It held! "Now if we can just keep it together until the workers bring in the materials to brace up the dam," he said.

So for the next few hours, Oogie rolled and patted, rolled and patted, and Ed picked up the balls and plugged the holes.

Finally the men arrived with the barrier and put it in place. Everyone cheered! "Whew!" thought Oogie. "A good job done!" He rode back to his mouse home on the toe of Ed's shoe. Beth ran alongside.

"We'll have a party tonight. This little dung beetle will be the guest of honor," Father announced, "He saved us all!"

That evening they all went down to the Fiesta Park, which was filled with all kinds of rides. The biggest one was a daring roller coaster that had twists and turns and climbed so very high!

"How'd you like to ride on that?" asked Ed.

Oogie thought, "How can he know this is just the adventure I need to make me famous!"

Oogie crawled under the end of a seat belt. Off he went, up, down, all around, upside down. Then up-up-up — oh so high. Then down he rushed. Oh he felt exhilarated!

Oogie could hardly wait to tell his friends and family about his adventurous ride. He would be famous! Great — wonderful — the only dung beetle ever to ride a roller coaster.

But, when you think about it, which deed really made Oogie famous? Saving the people from a broken dam or riding the roller coaster? You decide!

(Curious nature fact: You may think dung beetles gross, but it's a fact, without dung beetles, the earth would be piled high with manure!)

NOTES TO PARENTS:

You may want to ask your child for the answer to that question: which deed is more important? What kind of fame is short-lived? What kind of fame affects others in a way that is never forgotten? Who are the heros you know from your history books? What made them famous?

Just for Me!

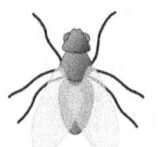

I am a common ordinary house fly. That is not exactly true. I am common, but I am not ordinary. In fact, I am extraordinary!

They call me Horace — Horace Fly. Not to be confused with a horse fly, which in truth is my cousin, who lives *with* his family in a barn and thrives on manure.

But I digress. That is, I'm off the track of what I was telling you.

I live on the porch of a very nice family, the Nelsons. There is Mother Nelson, Father Nelson, their son who is about twelve years old, and their daughter who is about four years old.

Oh yes, I mustn't forget their dog, a little Chihuahua named Pinki who, by the way, hates flies and loves to chase them.

My family lives on garbage and decaying things. Which is why I am so different — as I like only pieces of old jelly bread. I won't live long, two weeks to two months, but I will make the most of the time I have.

I never bite humans, but I love to torment Pinki. After I find a hole in the screen, I find Pinki, buzz her a few times, then take off and hide. Pinki barks, whines, and chases me.

When she sees me, she points her nose and stands very still, just like a hunting dog. Then I buzz her again and take off in another direction with Pinki in full pursuit, barking and whining.

Now to tell you about the night I became a hero.

I had decided to stay indoors and was resting on a small piece of jelly bread on the kitchen counter when I heard a loud snap, which came from the garage. A moment later, I smelled smoke!

I flew to the door to look through the keyhole and yes, smoke and little flames were coming from the garage.

I flew to the other side of the house where the bedrooms are, flew into the master bedroom where Father and Mother Nelson were sleeping, and I buzzed around Mr. Nelson's head a few times, but he brushed me aside. "Pesky fly," he said and promptly fell back to sleep.

I flew to the boy's bedroom. There was Pinki, snuggled at the foot of the bed. I buzzed her head, and she snapped at me with her jaw. I buzzed her again and she finally woke up fully.

Alert to the smell of smoke, Pinki danced around the bed, barking and whining. The boy awoke, smelled the smoke, grabbed his cell phone and ran to where his parents were sleeping, yelling, "Fire! Fire!"

Hearing this, Father Nelson awoke and remembered he was always prepared for emergencies — his bathrobe neatly folded on the nightstand, his slippers and a flashlight on top.

He grabbed the robe and put it on, then put on his slippers as he picked up the flashlight. In his Emergency Plan, he would have climbed out the bedroom window, but with his wife and children to think of, he changed the Plan.

Meanwhile, Mother Nelson put on her bathrobe and ran to her daughter's room to waken the little girl.

The Nelson boy had dialed 911 on his cell phone and, as calmly as possible, told the operator the problem and gave his address clearly, before hanging up.

The family dropped down to the floor where the smell of smoke was less dense and crawled to the front door and outside into the fresh air.

They heard the sirens and saw the fire engines coming down the street. The firefighters quickly sized up the situation and put out the fire. It had started in an outlet in the garage.

After airing out the house to rid it of smoke, the family bedded down for what was left of the night.

I spent the night on my little bit of jelly bread.

The next morning, Father Nelson remembered me — the fly that was trying to wake him. "That fly was trying to tell me about the fire," he told his family.

The next time I went to the kitchen, there was an extra big piece of jelly bread — just for me!

NOTES TO PARENTS:

Does your family have an Emergency Plan to use in case of a crisis or urgent situation? Do you have an escape plan in case of fire? A password for your child to use, if necessary? A plan to reconnect if a child is lost? Be sure that children memorize their address and phone number, as early as possible.

Bumble Bug

"I am lost," cried Jackie. "I don't know where I belong. Why, I'm not even sure what kind of bug I am! I know I started out being a cockroach. But our family grew so fast. There were so many of us, no room was left in the nest. Then the lady of the house saw me, picked up a newspaper, rolled it up, and hit me. Whack! And knocked me out. She threw me in the trashcan, and that's where I woke up. Well I couldn't very well go back to that house, could I? So I started walking."

Soon Jackie came upon a group of beetles called Dungs. My, they were busy bugs. Rolling. Patting. Rolling. Patting. "I can do that," said Jackie and quietly joined them. The Dungs were too busy to notice their new companion. Jackie rolled and patted. But the smell, oh the strong smell of the manure, got into her nostrils and choked her. This place was not for her, so she moved on.

When she came to a forest, she ventured in. It was dark and damp, a little too cold for her. "But I can make it," she said. She watched as the Earwig family headed toward an old fallen log. They crawled up under the bark, slid into a crevice, and fell asleep.

"I can do that," said Jackie, and she proceeded to crawl up under the bark where she tried to slip into a very small crevice. She didn't fit. She tried backing in; then she tried front first; she even tried sideways, but it was no use. Jackie was too big! "Well, I'll just find somewhere else," said the little cockroach.

Jackie walked out of the forest and through a field where she saw the large Grasshopper family hopping, hopping, hopping. "Why I know I can do that," said Jackie. She quickly joined in. Hop, hop, hop. But it wasn't as easy as it looked and became very tiring for a little roach. Jackie soon had her fill of this exercise, especially as the hoppers were not friendly towards her. She slipped away and walked on.

Coming upon an old shed, she slipped inside. Back in a dark corner she saw a large spider web with a very large spider sitting in the center waiting for its dinner to be caught in the web. "I can do that," said Jackie. She was just starting to climb onto the web when the big spider shouted, "No you don't. This is my web. You go spin your own!"

Jackie went to another corner of the shed. But try as she might, she could not produce a single strand. "Without spinnerets… I just can't do it." So Jackie moved on.

Outside she saw a parade of ants marching toward a large sand pile. Each one carried a bit of leaf or food crumb. One by one they dropped their food into the huge pile. "I can do that," said Jackie. And so she picked up a cookie crumb from the ground and joined in the march. After she dropped her crumb into the ant hole, she exclaimed, "Well, that was easy." When she noticed that the ants kept marching back down toward the picnic grounds across the field, Jackie followed them. She picked up another crumb and marched back. After about the third time, she was so tired she wailed, "Oh well, this is not for me!" and moved on.

When Jackie heard buzzing, she looked up. "It's bees!" she shouted, running toward the field of flowers where the bees had gathered to spread pollen and fill up with nectar. "I can fly, so I know I can do that," the little roach cried.

Up, up, she flew, across to the flowers but... once there what was she to do? She followed the bees back to their nest in the hollow tree. Some of them were doing a strange dance. "I can do that," she said.

But when she gave it a good try, the bees just laughed at her. "We are sending directions when we dance. We're telling the others which way to go with our movements," they told her. "You are just dancing... to dance."

So Jackie left the bees to their coded ways and sat down to think. She had tried many things: working the manure like dung beetles, hopping like the grasshoppers, spinning like the spiders, marching with the ants, soaring with the bees. She didn't fit in anywhere. "I guess you just have to be what you are meant to be," she concluded. "But what am I?"

Then a marvelous thought entered her tiny little head. "I know! I'll start a brand new species of insects! I'll call it the Bumble Bug. I'll be the best Bumble Bug that ever was! Or ever will be." And that she was.

NOTES TO PARENTS:

How does your child feel they fit into the family, their classroom, the world? Is there a special talent the child has that others may feel is "not valuable to society"? Ask your child to draw a Bumble Bug in the box with the question mark at the start of this story.

About the Author

Mary Dawn loves to tell stories. She started to tell stories to her dolls when she was a little girl. When she became a mother, she told stories to her children. When she became a grandmother, she told stories to grandchildren. And now to her great-grandchildren.

But she doesn't stop there. For many years, she told stories to her children's friends, who begged her to write them down. At last, she has.

You will find something in each story to talk about between parents and children — little known facts about insects and the ways they behave. Mary Dawn has one big message to pass on to all parents and children: Read to each other; read to yourself. Read! Read! Read!

Acknowledgments

This book is a gift produced by Mary Dawn's children and their families. Thanks to Monica for transposing the manuscript for computer use, to Val for editing and formatting, and to all the Justus kids for contributing to the success of this Buggy Project!

www.ingramcontent.com/pod-product-compliance
Lightning Source LLC
Chambersburg PA
CBHW071326130626
46556CB00004B/1768